What's for Breakfast?

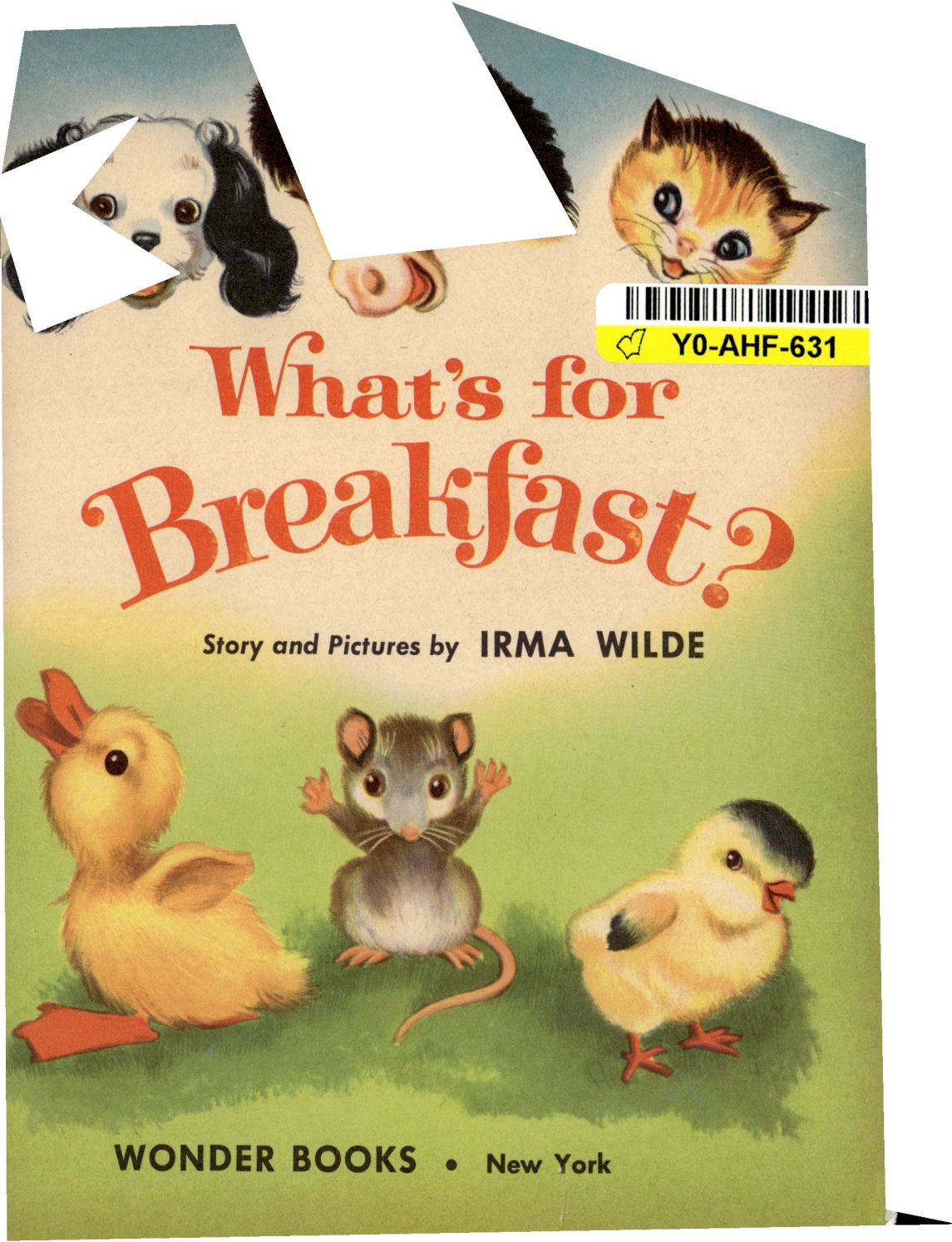

Story and Pictures by **IRMA WILDE**

WONDER BOOKS • New York

© 1950, by Wonder Books, Inc.
Originally published under the title *The Hungry Little Bunny*.
All rights reserved under International and Pan-American Copyright Conventions.
Published simultaneously in Canada.   Printed in the United States of America.

ONE MORNING Baby Bunny hopped out on the wrong side of the bed. This means that he was grumpy and grouchy and very contrary. He would not do anything his mother asked him to. He would not wash his face. He would not brush his long silky ears. He even would not eat his favorite breakfast of lettuce and carrots.

He pouted and fussed, and finally he pushed his breakfast bowl off the table. It fell on the floor with a loud crash!

"All right, Baby Bunny," said Mother Bunny. "You can find your breakfast somewhere else, and don't come home until you have learned how to behave."

This pleased Baby Bunny, and off he hopped. At first he wasn't quite sure where to go for his breakfast. Then he decided to have breakfast with the new Puppy on the farm. He hopped over to Farmer Green's barn to see the new Puppy.

"Good morning, Puppy," Baby Bunny said happily. "I've come to have breakfast with you."

"I just dug up a delicious bone," said the new Puppy. "You may have a chew."
"*No*, thank you," said Baby Bunny. "I don't care for old bones."

Kitty, who was near by, listening to Baby Bunny, said, "You can't have any of my cream, Baby Bunny. I want it all." Kitty was feeling a bit out of sorts herself.

"Well, I don't like cream, anyway," said Baby Bunny.

"Moo, moo," called out the Calf. "I've had my milk, and now I'm going to eat some hay, like a grown-up cow. Would you like some hay, Baby Bunny?"

"No, thank you," said Baby Bunny. "It tickles my nose."

"My oats won't tickle your nose, Baby Bunny," said the Foal. "Would you like some oats?"

"Oh dear, no," said Baby Bunny. "They aren't a bit crunchy."

"Oink, oink, oink," called out the Piglet. "I have some nice yellow corn on the cob. Would you like that, Baby Bunny?"

"Not for breakfast, thank you," Baby Bunny said.

"Baa, baa," said the baby Lamb. "These daisies are good for breakfast. They are nice and sweet. Won't you have some?"

"No, thank you, I don't eat flowers. They're too pretty," said Baby Bunny.

He hopped over to the pond nearby, and asked the Ducklings if he could have breakfast with them.

"Quack, quack, quack," the Ducklings said. "Come into the water with us. There are lots of good things to eat in the water."

"Oh no," said Baby Bunny. "I don't know how to swim. And I'm sure that I would not find anything to eat in the water."

"I think it will be better if you go home and ask your mother to give you your breakfast," the gentle Fawn told Baby Bunny. "Your mother knows what you like best. You tell her that you are hungry, and that you want your breakfast now. And be sure to say 'please.'"

"That is a wonderful idea," said Baby Bunny, with a happy little jump. "I would just love a nice bowl of lettuce and carrots for breakfast."

Off he skipped — hippety-hop, hoppety-hop — right up to his own house. Mother Bunny opened the door for him. "Hello, Baby Bunny," she said. "Did you have a good breakfast?" "No, Mother," said Baby Bunny, "I found out that a nice bowl of lettuce and carrots is the very best breakfast a hungry little bunny can eat."